MR. MEN LITTLE MISS Vets

Roger Hargreaves

Original concept by
Roger Hargreaves

Written and illustrated by
Adam Hargreaves

Little Miss Brainy was perfectly suited to being a vet.
She was clever.
She was kind.
She loved animals.
And she was patient.
Patient with her patients.

And patient with their owners!

Unlike Mr Grumpy who did not like animals.
And was most definitely not patient.

So, it was lucky that he was not a vet.

At the start of each new day, Little Miss Brainy never knew what kind of animal she would have to treat.

There were small animals.

And medium-sized animals.

And big animals!

"Really, Mr Wrong, it would be much better if I came to treat your bull at the farm!"

There were regular pets like cats and dogs
and hamsters and rabbits.

And there were exotic pets like snakes and spiders and frogs.

And then there were pets that were not animals.

Mr Nonsense was concerned about his pet rock. Which was a bit of a surprise, but Little Miss Brainy was able to reassure him that it was perfectly normal for a pet rock to stay so still.

Little Miss Brainy had a veterinary nurse to help her, Mr Quiet. He never knew what to expect from day to day. Sometimes he found the waiting room in mayhem.

Sometimes it was peaceful.

And sometimes it was just plain odd!

Like the time
a Cleverland pig
drove himself
to the surgery!

Little Miss Brainy had noticed that some of the pets were very like their owners.

Mr Bump's dog looked just like him once Little Miss Brainy had patched him up.

Little Miss Splendid's bird of paradise was just as splendid as she was.

Maybe even more so!

Mr Clumsy had a very shaggy dog.

Mr Tickle's python was as long and wriggly as his arms.

And Mr Greedy's cat was just as greedy as he was.

However, some owners were not like their pets ...

Mr Forgetful did not have a memory like his pet elephant!

Some days Little Miss Brainy had very puzzling visits.

Mr Silly brought in his cat. "I'm worried," he said. "My cat has been acting very strangely of late."

"Woof!" barked the cat.

"Gosh! That is very peculiar," said Little Miss Brainy, with concern.

"Oh, that's perfectly normal," explained Mr Silly. "All cats bark in Nonsenseland. No, the problem is that she's stopped burying bones."

There wasn't a cure for that.

Little Miss Naughty brought in her parrot.

A parrot who said very naughty, rude things.

There wasn't a cure for that either.

And Little Miss Quick brought in her pet tortoise. "He's too slow. He can't keep up with me," complained Little Miss Quick.

And, again, there wasn't a medical cure for that.

Although, Little Miss Brainy did have one suggestion.

Sometimes people brought in injured wild animals.

Little Miss Tiny brought in a robin with an injured wing which needed a splint.

And Mr Strong brought in a weasel with a wounded foot
which needed to be cleaned and bandaged.

Mr Small brought in a hedgehog with a nasty cold.
The hedgehog needed some medicine.

And Little Miss Stubborn brought in an animal in a box. "This snail has lost its shell," she announced.

Little Miss Brainy examined the snail. "This isn't a snail, it's a slug."

"Nonsense!" cried Little Miss Stubborn. "I know a shell-less snail when I see one."

"I assure you, it's a slug," said Little Miss Brainy.

"No, it's a snail."

Little Miss Brainy sighed. It was going to be a long day.

It could be hard work being a vet. Animals didn't always fall ill during the day, there were times they needed attention at night.

Like Farmer Field's flock of sheep during lambing time.

They kept Little Miss Brainy up all night.

But it was all made worthwhile seeing the lambs skipping about in the morning.

There was a swimming pool at the vets. It was used to help animals recuperate from their injuries.

Mr Quiet was helping a horse with a broken leg to exercise in the pool.

The Cleverland pig had other ideas about how the pool ought to be used.

Now and then Little Miss Brainy had to perform an operation.

Like the time Mr Muddle's pet duck swallowed a bone. But that wasn't all Little Miss Brainy found.

She also removed a ball and a whistle and a squeaky toy.

Perhaps Mr Muddle's duck is as muddled-up as its owner!

Little Miss Brainy also got called out to the zoo where she had to treat a rhinoceros with a broken horn.

A hippopotamus
with tummy ache.

A grizzly bear with a headache.

A tiger with toothache.

A crocodile with backache.

And a giraffe with neckache!

"You must have treated every sort of animal on the planet," said the zoo keeper.

"I certainly have," laughed Little Miss Brainy. "I don't think there's anything that could surprise me. I've had pet rocks and barking cats and Cleverland pigs and shell-less snails!"

Now, just between you and me, Little Miss Brainy may have spoken too soon.

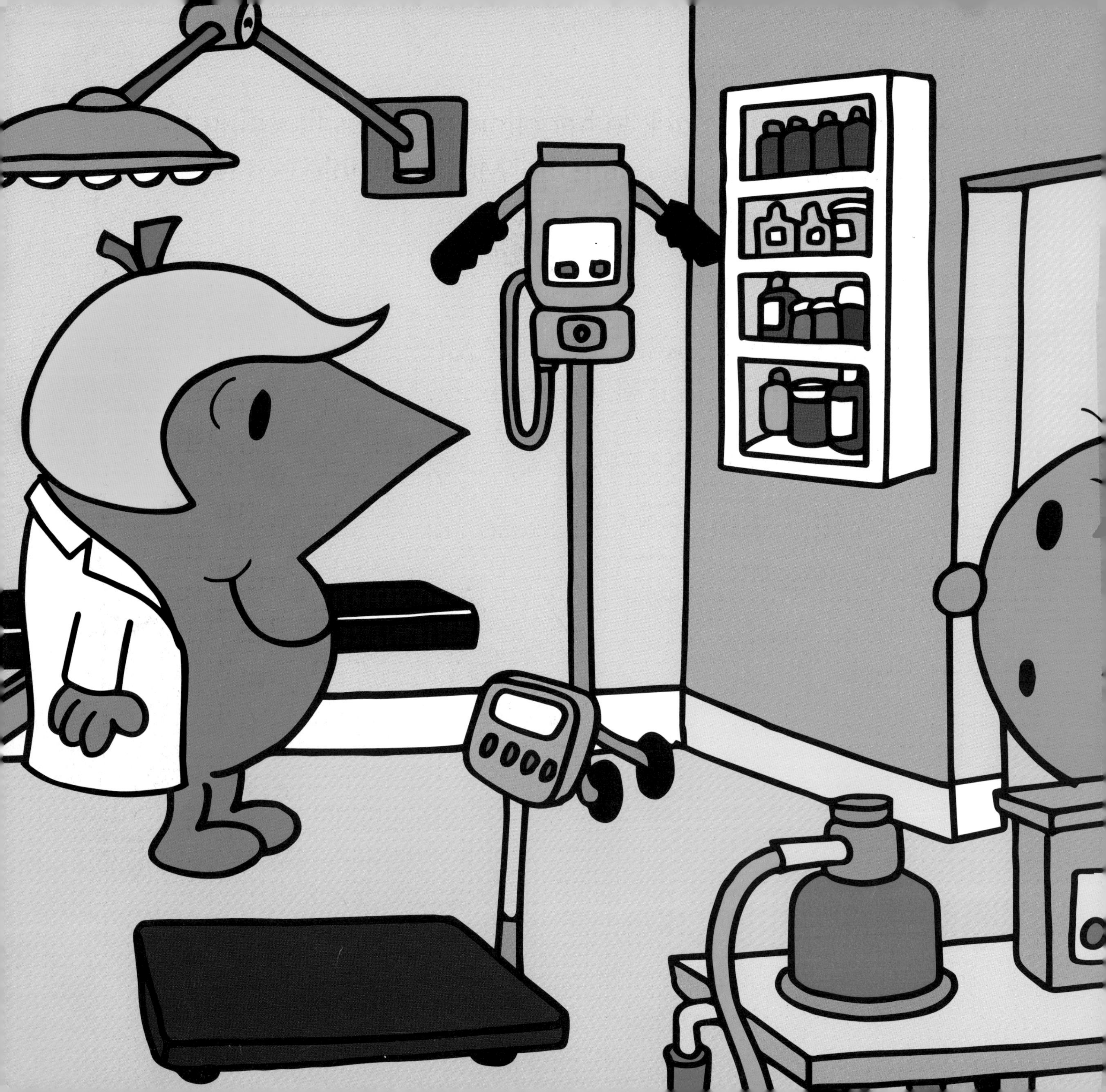

Little Miss Brainy went back to her clinic and was finishing up for the day when Mr Quiet came in. "Mr Impossible has just brought in his pet, its teeth need cleaning."

"Send him in," said Little Miss Brainy.

"That won't be so easy," grimaced Mr Quiet. "In fact, you'll need to do it in the car park."

So, Little Miss Brainy went outside.

Mr Impossible's pet was more than a little unusual.

A lot more than a little.

It was a Tyrannosaurus rex!

Now, that was a surprise.

A big surprise!